Sleeping Beauty

A PARRAGON BOOK

Published by
Parragon Books,
Unit 13–17, Avonbridge Trading Estate,
Atlantic Road, Avonmouth, Bristol BS11 9QD

Produced by
The Templar Company plc,
Pippbrook Mill, London Road, Dorking, Surrey RH4 1JE

Designed by Mark Kingsley-Monks

Printed and bound in Italy

ISBN 0-75250-793-1

Sleeping Beauty

Retold by Caroline Repchuk
Illustrated by Alison Winfield

‖ •PARRAGON• ‖

Once upon a time there lived a King and Queen who longed to have a child. At last the Queen had a daughter, and there was great rejoicing throughout the land. She was a sweet little Princess, and her parents named her Briar-Rose. The day of her christening arrived, and everyone came from far and wide to celebrate the great occasion.

Seven fairies were chosen to be godmothers, and came dressed in their most beautiful clothes.

After the ceremony, the King and

Queen and all their guests returned
to the Palace for a great feast.

"Health and happiness," they cried,
toasting the little Princess.

Suddenly there was a crash as the Palace door flew open. In the doorway stood a wizened old woman. She was an ancient fairy who had not been seen for many years.

"Why was I not invited to the christening?" demanded the old crone angrily, pointing to the beautiful baby as she lay in her cot. The frightened queen explained that no one in the court realised that she was still alive, but that she was most welcome to join them at the banquet table.

After the feast it was time for the fairies to give their presents to the little Princess.

The first six gave her beauty, wisdom, grace, dancing feet, a lovely voice and the gift of music.

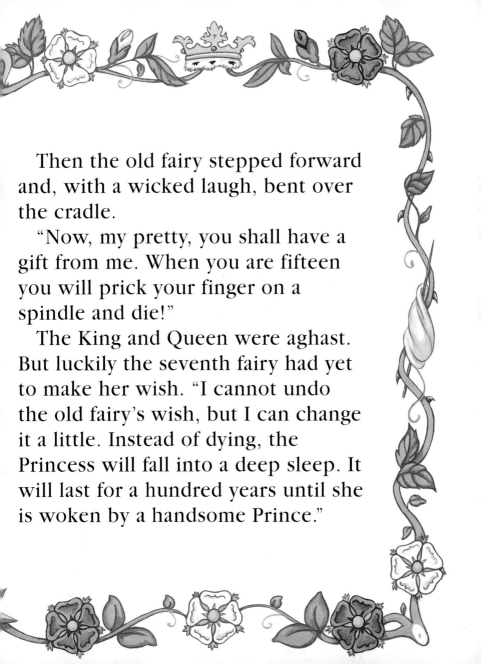

Then the old fairy stepped forward and, with a wicked laugh, bent over the cradle.

"Now, my pretty, you shall have a gift from me. When you are fifteen you will prick your finger on a spindle and die!"

The King and Queen were aghast. But luckily the seventh fairy had yet to make her wish. "I cannot undo the old fairy's wish, but I can change it a little. Instead of dying, the Princess will fall into a deep sleep. It will last for a hundred years until she is woken by a handsome Prince."

Time passed, and gradually the King and Queen forgot all about the wicked fairy and her terrible wish. And so Princess Briar-Rose grew into a beautiful young girl.

One day, on her fifteenth birthday, the young Princess was exploring the Palace and found a narrow staircase that she had never seen before. Behind a small door, was a little room where an old woman sat spinning. "What are you doing?" asked the curious Princess.

"Spinning, child," said the old woman, not knowing who she was. The Princess asked to take a closer look but, as she touched the spindle, the needle pricked her finger, and she fell in a dead faint to the floor.

The old woman cried out in alarm, and people came rushing from all directions, but no one could wake the lovely Princess.

Then the King remembered the old fairy's wish, and knew that his daughter would now stay asleep for a hundred long years.

He ordered his courtiers to carry her to the finest room in the palace, where she could sleep quietly until her hour of awaking arrived. She looked very beautiful, as she lay there breathing softly.

When the good seventh fairy heard the news, she hurried to the palace. She had another important spell to make.

With a wave of her wand, she put
every other living thing to sleep
along with the Princess, so that in a

hundred years time, they would all
wake together. Within minutes, a deep
silence had fallen over the Palace.

In an instant a hedge of thorns grew up around the Palace walls. It was so thick that nothing could pass through it.

And so a hundred years passed slowly by, and inside the thorny hedge nothing stirred.

Then one day a handsome young Prince came riding by and saw the Palace towers rising up behind the hedge. One of his courtiers told him that a beautiful Princess was said to lie inside, trapped in a deep sleep. The Prince felt strangely drawn towards the Palace, and stepped into the thick thorn hedge. To his surprise the branches parted to let him through, and he reached the Palace without a scratch.

But as he stepped into the courtyard, he gasped to see the dreadful sight of men, women and animals stretched out upon the ground, looking just as if they were dead. As he moved closer, however, he could see that they were only sleeping.

Quickly the Prince entered the Palace and ran through room after room, each full of sleeping figures.

At last he came to a magnificent chamber and there, lying fast asleep on the bed, was the Princess.

The Prince had never seen such a beautiful sight, and instantly he fell in love. He leant over the bed and gently kissed the lovely Princess.

At once the spell was broken, and the Princess slowly opened her eyes. She blushed shyly when she saw the handsome Prince leaning over her. "You have found me at last, my Prince," she said.

On bended knee the Prince asked her to marry him, and to his joy, she agreed.

In every corner figures were stretching and yawning, as slowly the Palace came back to life. Great was the rejoicing when the Royal Wedding was announced.

And so the Sleeping Beauty and her Prince were married, and lived happily ever after.

CHARLES PERRAULT

The Sleeping Beauty, or *La Belle au bois dormant* was written by the French poet and storyteller, Charles Perrault (1628-1703) and was first published in 1696. The following year it was included in his collection of fairy stories which brought together many traditional folk tales, including *Puss in Boots, Little Red Riding-Hood* and *Cinderella* and together they became known as *Mother Goose's Tales*. Written in a simple unaffected style, Perrault's stories quickly became popular in France and later throughout the world. *The Sleeping Beauty* first appeared in English in 1729. In a later version, written by the Brothers Grimm, the Princess was named Briar-Rose and the original gruesome ending was amended. Now, instead of the wicked mother-in-law instructing that the grandchildren should be cooked for supper, the story ends happily with the Princess awakening and marrying her Prince!